T0368695

The Mysterious Neighbors 2

CINDY PARCELLS

authorHOUSE®

AuthorHouse™
1663 Liberty Drive
Bloomington, IN 47403
www.authorhouse.com
Phone: 833-262-8899

Published by AuthorHouse 12/27/2024

ISBN: 979-8-8230-4001-3 (sc)
ISBN: 979-8-8230-4000-6 (e)

Library of Congress Control Number: 2019909926

Print information available on the last page.

This book is printed on acid-free paper.

Madison High School

The end of summer was coming soon. Registration for 9th grade at Madison High School was next Tuesday. "Catherine, "Ben's mom said, "As the wise saying goes, "when you start to get older time begins to fly by." She was right thought Ben, summer seemed to go by so fast. A few trips up to Henry's cottage and visiting my grandparents in Traverse City, Michigan was awesome. But the best two things I did with my family and friends was to go back up to see Mackinaw Island, riding bikes for eight miles around the Island, and taking the ferry boat under the Mackinaw bridge seeing all the great architecture up close. Lastly, of course, I loved organizing the new Junior Detective Club.

Starting the Junior Detective Club kept us all so busy. Opening applications, letters, sending out club denial letters and acceptance letters. We did not notice the outdoors, what time it was or even what day it was we were so busy. Ben's mom made us lunches, sub sandwiches, peanut butter and jelly and bags of chip and pop or Gatorade to drink.

"Ben said out loud, "This club is going to be much bigger, busier and possibly a huge money- making club than I ever dreamed about. Many kids are being put on waiting lists for next year or even two years from now. Some kids are being added to a smaller club that Parker ad Henry may watch over. Henry's parents have a cottage up in Harbor Beach, Michigan, a three- hour drive away from Madison. There have been many new cottages built near the water and a nearby wooded area.

"Jenny and Josh were a year younger in school than Parker and Henry and I. Henry and Parker were the two magicians on the computers. They made spectacular spreadsheets, stored addresses, names, street names and suspicious locations in the city of Madison and northern city of Harbor Beach. High school was so exciting for Parker, Henry and I, Josh and Jenny were in their final year at Madison Middle school. Josh was the best forward on the school soccer team. Jenny was top chair in the jazz band playing clarinet. Parker and I were also in Robotics club and computer club. They both have received many awards for their advanced computer skills. We ere lucky to have a few of our classes together. Parker and Henry were in each other's English I class and also Computer technology class. "I was in Spanish and Algebra II class."" Math came easy for Parker. My favorite class was History. Jenny loved playing the Clarinet and she was really good in her English class. Jenny always had a book of some kind open, reading late into the night.

Junior Detective Beginnings

Jenny, Josh and I sorted out teams of 4 to survey different sections of our city of Madison. The north side was near the high school, the east side was the middle school zone. The park area was the west side and the south was near the elementary school. Those night vision binoculars would sure come in handy up north. We had not thought of the kits for up north or even for near the creepy boarded up house. Now that we feel safe knowing the police are just a call away and can protect us if things get too scary or unsafe.

As I explained at the first meeting to the new members, the junior detective club is mostly for fun, learning, friendships and safety of our town and the up-north city of Harbor Beach, Michigan. Many of our classmates were turned away due to non-history of family police work. Our 9th grade class was a very large class. It had two hundred and fifty students in our graduating class. We had our meetings at the park every Friday afternoon at 4:00.

The areas of the city were now broken up into four to

six members for each area plus up north. All parts of the city would now be covered north, south, east and west. Monthly dues of twenty-five dollars would be collected by Ben, Jenny, Parker, Josh or Henry. We would each lead and teach the groups of new members in each area. The member fees would include usage of the detective kits, special headlights, dayglo orange and green vests with initials JDC on each vest. Uncle Al and Jerry added in the headlights and vests for safety. One final donation to the club was from the captain, fleece gloves one size fits all for winter days and cool night usage. Again, these gloves would be great up-north. It can get extremely cold in northern Michigan.

These donations were so awesome for our new club. "I would have to have all the leaders of the club write a special letter of thanks to our Uncle Al and Jerry for these super additions to our detective work and keeping our city a safe and welcoming neighborhood for families to feel safe, to live, enjoy parks, biking, hiking and community fun in our city. "I am so glad I thought of this, said Ben to Jenny.

"I have never heard of any group of kids put together in any other city like this. "I think we are one of the first groups of teens to watch over our city and up-north vacationing lake city such as Harbor Beach. Families are large, busy and don't often think of crime that may be happening in their town right next door. "Yes, like last summer helping Uncle Al and Jerry put away criminals that have been on the loose for such a long, long time was a great accomplishment. Scary, fun, and busy at times but well worth every, cold sometimes snowy night and days spent trying to solve our first actual neighborhood crime. Who knows what will happen this year and from now on with kids always ready to learn, solve mysteries and even go into criminal justice or police work when they graduate school and college?" "I had so much fun last summer discovering the neighbors, using the detective night vision binoculars, magnifying glasses, and notebooks. "I was really feeling special and also learning a lot about police and detective work." "Well Jen, I know I am young but getting my feet wet, so to speak in detective work is really nothing better for me." "This is my chosen college major most definitely either some sort of detective work, police work will happen in my near future."

Jenny said you are really serious and determined, awesome Jenny said to find your passion at 14. "I love playing the clarinet and reading, I believe is my real passion. "I think I want to become either an English teacher a writer." There is still time but I know one of these will lead me to happiness at the end of high school. "Detective work is exciting and fun, but I don't seem to have a lot of time to help out this year with soccer, jazz band and my love of reading." Hurting my ankle really slowed me down. It took a while to help with the Junior detective club."

"That's okay we have a lot of new members now, and we may not run into any problems or cases to watch over or work on." You never know what is out there to find. Madison seemed like a normal city, but you never know what is lurking behind a closed door or even in someone's backyard, as we found out."

3

Homework, Homework, Homework

Our ninth- grade classes began after the first two weeks homework began to pile up. We never realized, tests, reports would happen so soon in the school year. Henry was keeping up with delivery of the local city newspaper, every Thursday morning. They're was a creepy old house boarded up and hanging roof shingles falling off on his route. The house always looked abandoned. A dim light shown through a cracked basement window and loud clicking noises and a funny odor was coming from the house. As Henry got off his bike and tossed the paper to the porch on the lawn appeared to be two twenty- dollar bills falling out of a bag. Henry knocked on the door assuming the owner dropped this bag of twenty-dollar bills by accident. Knocking at the door and ringing the bell for at least ten times, no one answered the door. Well he would come back after school and try again to return it. The name on the paper order was Jim Jones. Suddenly, a man came out from the backyard. "Oh, said Henry are you Mr. Jones."?

"I am the UPS man delivering packages." "I don't live here." "The man requested all packages be delivered to the back porch only."

The next week Josh was riding through the edge of the park on his way to soccer practice. As he looked down, he thought it was some sort of garbage to be thrown away but, as he looked closer, he jumped off his bike and said out loud. Oh my gosh he could not believe his eyes. "No way what is this a fifty- dollar bill, no more three more scattered amongst leaves on the ground!!!Two hundred dollars, wow he thought. He looked around for someone who may have lost or dropped these bills. No one was near accept the woods and the creepy old house. I knocked on the door to see if the owner was home, no one answered. Josh noticed an odor of oil, ink he could not make out the smell and the same clicking noise Henry had told to Ben and Jen. I better put these bills back in the bag and remember to tell Ben at the next meeting. I did not know if the man at this house lost them. I know if I dropped some money I would hope to get it returned to me. This money also had a funny fresh smell that same odor that was coming from near the house. No cars were ever there many times I have rode my bike by it always looks abandoned. Loud noises and constant odor are always coming from around the house. This creepy old house is right against the entrance to the woods. It always seems dark accept lights coming from the basement window. I will relay this info to Ben at the first meeting of our Junior Detective Club group.

4

Fall Cottage Closing

Harbor Beach, Michigan was getting very cold in the late fall. There was a real icy cold wind blowing and most of the leaves were off the trees. "We usually close up our cottage much earlier in the fall season, but my dad has been traveling for his job." Traveling takes up a lot of my dad, Peters, time lately to do much closing of the cottage here in Harbor Beach. We have had our cottage for 6 years now. Boating, swimming and visiting relatives in the area is a super great time away from our every day lives. I was proud and excited to always go boating and come up north to be with friends, family and nature. We have to close up our cottage every fall, because we have no heat in the winter. I guess it is called and year-around cottage and we open in May and close by early November. The snow comes early in the north of Michigan.

Parker was asked to come up to enjoy the last few days of the cottage and help us close up. Raking up leaves, clearing gutters on the ladders of leaves, mostly done by my dad was quite a project.

Henry and Parker decided to take a break and get one last look at the beach area and lake- Huron. "Clear as a bell, Henry said." "My dad says that many times when we come up to the cottage." We noticed a few separate smaller enclosed screened in cottages. Walking past we both heard low growling, moaning noises. There were no lights on in the enclosed cottage. No one seemed to be around. We did not want to get too close. The screens on the cottage appeared to be open a crack. Even with our special night binoculars and goggles we could not see in to find out the strange noises.

As we walked further down near the water, we both heard some more weird and strange animal like noises. The noises were coming from another small cottage near the woods behind the property next door. The noises were very hard to hear almost donkey like squealing and loud snorts like maybe a horse. Very strange and unusual.

Henry and I knocked on the main cottage door. It was located at the very end of the property way down back by the lake front. No one answered they looked to be also, closed up for the winter. No lights on, curtains and blinds closed. "Hmmm Henry said." "let's go back one more time and listen and try to figure out the sounds. We noticed large locks on the doors and even the screened windows. "No one could enter or even exit it looked like to us, very strange and kind of creepy." "Thinking, what animals or even if they were animals inside the small cottages, why was not no one around? Was this legal and even cruel to be left alone in this cold and soon to be snowing northern property.?"

Remembering back 3 months ago, Henry and I remember similar noises, last summer, but never thought much about it then." "Thinking maybe dogs, wolves or some other animal in the woods, maybe being up north, no big deal." "Maybe we should get out our notebooks and write dates down, sounds, and the location down to tell Ben and the others at Friday's meeting. As we circled the cottages sometimes the noises would stop, other times they would be louder and sometimes very frightening noises."

It was time to get back home wrapping of dishes, boxing up food that could be used within 3-4 months, cereal, crackers, pasta, soup cans, and paper goods all put away up high in a deep kitchen pantry in Mrs. King's kitchen. Blankets, beach towels, swim suits, shorts and clothing all stored in boxes in a hall closet. "Well said Peter, Mr. King looks like we are all set for winter." "Let's go out for a big breakfast in town and head home, Thanksgiving was in two weeks." We stopped at the Harbor Beach Diner. We all had different types of pancakes. Henry and I had a big stack of chocolate chip pancakes with a side of bacon and large glass of orange juice. Mrs. King had French toast and coffee and Mr. King loved omelets, with a small side of pancakes. We were all filled to the rim, so to speak. "Delicious Parker said, and thank you very much for breakfast and the fun trip up north." "Thank you, said Mr. King you helped us a lot, raking leaves repairing trouble on our computers and storing things away." "A cottage is a lot of work and responsibility, but well worth the boating, relaxation and get-a-way time."

I'm hoping we can find an inside place to meet, it is becoming really cold outside", said Parker. Thinking to himself Henry could not mention the noises yet to his parents. Maybe, they were nothing to worry about, but again I think this will be a great conversation to have with Ben and the Junior detective club at the next meeting.

We were getting home about dinner time and Mr. King decided to stop at our favorite pizza spot near home Alibi Pizza. "Awesome said Henry, thanks Dad." "We have not had this pizza in so long." "It is getting late and I think we all worked up a big appetite most of Saturday packing, cleaning and wrapping up the pipes for winterization of the cottage." Two large pizzas and Lemonade and my mom wanted a large Antipasto salad that was so delicious we could hardly wait for our order to come to the table.

We arrived at the house about 7:30 and decided to play a few games of Uno and then my parents joined us and we played Euchre. Euchre is played in pairs and can be challenging but so fun to play. Parker and I teamed up and we beat my parents 2 games to 1. It was almost ten at night and it was getting tired. Parker only lived 6 houses down the street so he took his suitcase and treats he bought up north and arrived home. What a weekend, fun, fast and surely mysterious.

Dreaming of all the sounds and noises and deer we saw I fell asleep remembering about Grandpa Jerry's antler collection. He was a big deer hunter when he was younger. He grew up in a small town called Evart in northern Michigan. My family owned 4 acres of land behind their house. He fished and mostly hunted deer. His prized collection of deer antlers hung up and displayed on a plaque in his basement in Traverse City.

But his real joy was his largest deer and head of antlers on the wall. This deer was huge a rack of 10 points. The biggest antler rack I ever saw. As I dozed off into a deep well- deserved sleep.

5

Holiday Break

The final meeting at the park was at 3:00 after school. Josh and Henry presented reports of finding money. Peculiar and strange money- in baggies. "Ben told the others everyone on all teams be on the lookout for bags of money on the ground. This is an unusual thing to be happening one person finding money but two people.? This may be a case developing before our eyes. "Ben said out loud, "remember Jenny when Uncle Al and Jerry told us "don't count anything out and whatever you do never use the evidence, or suspicious bags or packages." "Keep them in a safe place for a while in case more show up or it leads into something mysterious happening in the area." Twenties and fifty- dollar bills in bags near the edge of the park entrance trail and the creepy boarded up house. We also heard each of us at different times, banging and clicking noises. "One other thing Henry said," a very funny odor coming from near the house on the side of the house where the crack in the basement window was found". "Either oil, gas or even a type of heavy ink smell."

Parker and Henry brought up some mysterious news from near Henry's cottage. "The neighbors next door had a large cottage with 2-3 other smaller ones. "Two or three times we heard noises as we walked near them, and no one seemed to be around living in the main cottage."

Summer was fun at Henry's cottage. We went boating, tubing, swimming, hiking and sight- seeing, said Hunter. Hearing strange animal noises without anyone around seemed very weird. We thought we might see or hear animal pet noises, maybe a cat or dog. There were three cottages. One large cottage or small building near the edge of the lake, and two other smaller ones near the edge of the woods trail.

Henry's cousin Tom has worked and lived in Harbor Beach for 15 years, he has been a detective in town for at least 10 years. We decided, Parker and I to report this information to him just as a precaution. Last year Henry remembered hearing noises also mostly in the summer and fall. Tom Henry's cousin told us to just keep watching and being aware of the noises, when, what type of noises and neighbors being at the cottage or not. He had a heavy workload this summer being in the animal cruelty department kept him constantly busy. Being up-north has tons of animal cruelty problems, unfortunately. Tom told the boys that animal cruelty of any kind was aloud. I will have a patrol car drive through the area in question towards the end of the fall and on and off this winter just to make sure all seems okay. Tom told us, better be safe than sorry. He also said, although the woods are highly populated with every animal possible, these sounds you two have been hearing are not your average wildlife sounds even up in this neck of the woods.

Thanksgiving was in two days and the leaves were already beginning to fall off the trees. It really was feeling like winter was right around the corner, even down here in Madison, Michigan.

As discussed at the last meeting at the park, we will move them inside to Ben and Jenny's basement. It would be very full now with 25 members. It will work out and be much better than a cold snowy park in the coming winter.

Some of the new members that were put on the northern, Harbor Beach team, decided to drop out. These 12 members were very involved in clubs. Science club, computer club, swim team and basketball teams. They all thought they would have time to join in the junior detective club. The Harbor Beach team is for now only Henry, Parker and a few more kids that have cottages in the surrounding area.

All of the Junior-Detective Club will be spending Christmas and holiday vacation with family. The detective club also closed until mid-January. Everyone was glad to have a break from the club and from school.

6

A New Year

Another surprise was given to the group, fleece gloves 40 pair. Captain Smith of the Madison Police Department was a super -man. "Wow", said Ben so awesome. Our hands will be so warm now as we bike or hike and survey these mysterious neighbors. Especially using these gloves for the Harbor Beach area Cottages.

Catherine, Ben and Jenny's mom made up a list of things she needed at the hardware store. Ben's dad was out of town on business and his mom Catherine had to get a root canal done on her tooth at the dentist. She knew a trip to the hardware store would not be possible after the root canal was done.

Jenny has had a walking cast on her left foot for three weeks now. She badly sprained her ankle scoring a winning goal over a month ago. "I feel terrible not to be able to bike and help with the detective club." Said Jenny. "That's okay Ben said, accidents happen." It's nice to be able to walk now with my walking cast. I want to get some fresh air it's a nice sunny day. The doctor said its good to walk and strengthen my ankle. As we were getting near the store, we noticed police cars surrounding the hardware store. Inside as we gathered light bulbs, garbage kitchen bags, paint rollers and bunches of lawn bags, I noticed a policeman using a special lighted wand scanning over money at the register.

Jenny over-heard two policemen talking to the manager about funny money, or otherwise known to most as counterfeit money being used at the store. They continued to check all paper bills passing through the store, using a new wand with a special blue light that shows a seal to prove its real money. If no seal is found on the bill the money is fake, or printed up on a special printing machine producing bills in any amount. So far fifty-dollar bills were counterfeit as were a few twenty-dollar bills used in the store. So said the policeman to the manager your store employees will have to scan all monies used to purchase any items in the store from now on. As Jenny and Ben's eyes almost popped out their head and their mouths fell open hearing this news, Ben could not believe what they were hearing. Ben went to pay for his mom's items on the list. "Uh-Oh" Ben said, as he pulled out a bag full of fifty-dollar bills Josh found near the creepy boarded house. He forgot to take this out of his inside pocket of his winter coat. The meeting was a few weeks ago and I switched coats because of the cooler weather. Hey Ben said to Jenny, we should get this money checked out by the wand." Yeah, said Jenny maybe we should get it looked at now. We will have to tell the policemen who we are and how we found the money. As we proceeded to tell them we are the Junior Detective Club kids for the city of Madison and Harbor Beach Michigan. Also, our Uncle Al and Jerry worked for the police department for a long time. Bingo! "there were no seals on any of the bills in our bag." They would hold onto the money for us and if we found more, which we have we will get it checked out very soon. They told us to survey the surrounding are of the house and let them know if any more money is found.

7

Discoveries at the Creepy House

Henry had an idea! While delivering papers on his morning route, he decided to see if those packages at the creepy house were still on the back porch. Nope, no packages were on the back porch that the ups man delivered. So, someone must be living there Henry thought to himself. Henry knocked on a few neighbors door later that day. The morning delivery of the paper is at 6:30 a.m. He did not want to wake neighbors up so early in the morning.

Before Josh's soccer game later that day Josh and Henry knocked on a few neighbor's doors and no neighbors ever seen or have heard anyone coming or going from that house. They too heard loud clicking machine noises. One neighbor walks her dog late at night after work and she occasionally smelled a funny odor coming from the area.

On the way home from the hardware store Ben and Jenny had to walk through the woods, a short-cut to get to their house. The woods made the walk shorter by three blocks from the hardware store. So much garbage was found, litterbugs, Jenny said. Wait, said Jenny taking a look at the bags. Digging through the bag she found four, one hundred-dollar bills. Really, said Ben. Look over here another bag, two one hundred- dollar bills inside the blue bags. Another bag with three fifty-dollar bills were in a green bag, and twenty-dollar bills were in an orange bag. This is getting stranger and stranger. Yeah, said Ben we better put all these bags together and soon tell the police about the money bags, odor and strange clicking machine noises coming from the creepy trail house.

The next meeting was in three days. Ben decided to ask Jenny, Josh, Parker, and Henry to all meet up at the park. The weather was beginning to get warmer as spring was on its way here. It would be on a Saturday late afternoon. Ben told the four leaders to bring their black gloves, night-time binoculars, and cameras. The junior detective club did not want to be noticed. They wore their day-glow lime green vests over dark coats. Just in-case they were seen by nosy neighbors or questioned. Junior detective credentials would show who they were if reported. The city police would know who these kids were and not be prosecuted. Ben wanted to stay as hidden as possible it was almost eight and getting dark outside. Two at a time they would survey and watch the property and the house. No movement anywhere for twenty-minutes. Just familiar loud clanging machine running noises. Two of them ran over to the creepy boarded up house and peeked in the cracked basement window.

Henry ran around the back of the house. Henry turned on his flashlight on low-beam and saw a bag from the Madison Hardware. Taking out his camera, Parker took four pictures of what looked like a bag of receipts. Bolts, screws, wrenches, special copy paper, and a separate receipt. A large bottle of black ink used for printing it said on the bottle. This was no ordinary bottle it was probably five gallons of ink something very hard to lift. His binoculars helped him read the receipt, credit card number and a name of Jim Jones. That's it, said Parker he must be the man who lives here.

As Josh, Henry and Parker ran this bag from the back porch over to Ben, he put the receipts in his detective bag for his Uncle Al. They regrouped and Ben told them to look around for a car, a bike, a truck or even a motorcycle. This property was huge. Immaculate trimmed bushes and gardens surrounding the house. I think this house is the biggest in the city of Madison. By the time we checked out the whole yard, it was almost nine at night, and we could hardly see anything. Thank goodness for our headlights, Parker turned his on as did the rest of us, great light, but not too bright. He was in the furthest bushy area from the house. He saw a large tarp hanging from the biggest oak tree he ever saw. We all helped pull it back and down. A motorcycle and a bike with a large basket on the front and back of the bike. "Wow this is where he hides his vehicles, said Parker. Well this is probably enough information to collect for now, said Ben. As soon as we get home Ben was going to remember to write down all of the things we saw, found and of course, time and date and locations. This creepy house is a mystery. We have to keep observing it and find out what the noises are coming from and the particular odor we are smelling. The odor really seems to be getting stronger and stronger every time we come over to this creepy boarded up house.

8

Spring Opening in Harbor Beach

It was Easter break for the schools in Madison. Henry and Parker were excited to come up north to explore Harbor Beach and help open up the cottage for a few seasons. Henry's dad went up three hours earlier to get the heat turned on and put wood in their fire to help warm the cottage. It can get really cold up-north over the winter.

Catherine, Henries mom, Henry and Parker just arrived in Harbor beach just after noon. Henry and Parker wanted to stretch their legs, so they took a walk to explore the outdoors. As they got near one of the cottage's they heard loud growling animal noises. This is the third time, I have heard these noises, said Henry, and each time no one seemed to be around. There were a few boats tied up rather large boats almost like they were for transporting big and large objects. Henry ran back to get his camera. I think I need a picture of these two boats they are really big and unusual. No roof tops, extremely large boats and the size of the motors were very big not one motor but three motors side-by-side on each boat. Looking further at the boats there were open air crates for transporting something. We were right maybe these people were up to no good. I have never seen this large of boat on Lake Huron in my life and I have been around a lot of boats, said Parker. I think I will take a picture of the name of the boats and license numbers just for safety reasons. Orange Crush was one name and Animal Lover was another name. Another cottage that was near the lake had lower bird like sounds coming from that cottage. The cottages were always dark, and all three had very different possible animal noises coming from inside each one of the cottages. We will note all this information down in our notebooks to report back to Ben and the rest of the Junior Detective Club next week after spring break was over.

9

Hardware Surveillance

Ben is watching the hardware store. He has had a feeling or a gut instinct that he really is good at following. Behind a bush near the hardware been is hiding to take pictures and notes of this strange man riding a red colored bike with a front basket and a rear basket attached. Yes, he thought this is probably the same bike we found under that tarp at the creepy house that night. Jim Jones that must be him. He had a long scraggly beard, holy jeans, a black hat and coat and carrying colored bags all bundled together. He was very shaky on the bike and looked very nervous or scared. This guy is sure hiding something and I won't stop surveying his house and him until we figure out this mysterious creepy house happenings.

Jenny sees people with colored bags at the mall all the time. Similar to the bags we have found and Jim Jones is carrying. Probably a coincidence, but maybe not thought Ben. Ben can not stop thinking about these strange happenings with the colored bags. I have been doing so much lately. Jenna reminded Ben how busy he has been. Not getting enough rest because of soccer, swim team meets, homework and constantly walking, or biking surveying suspicious areas for the Club. She is probably right my mind has been working overtime and I need to take a few days off from all activities and refuel my mind and body.

After resting up and feeling much better Ben goes on another quest to check around the hardware. Exactly at three pm on Tuesdays and Thursdays right after school Ben notices that bearded man Jim Jones biking either from or away from the hardware store with colored bags tied together almost dropping from his hands. The look on his face could tell a thousand words, something is up and I bet he is carrying different amounts of money in each of the bags like we found at the park trail. He must be delivering or receiving money from or through the hardware somehow. This mystery is becoming bigger and bigger. I won't rest until this man and creepy mystery house gets solved thinks Ben.

Through emails and texting with Ben and Jenny's cousin Jonathan read the messages he was receiving from them. Loving his ideas and new detective club sleuthing Jonathon decides to start a club a few months ago in Cincinnati, Ohio. Since his Uncle Jerry used to live and work on the police force their he was safe to start his own club. Keeping close email contact with his cousins Jen and Ben his excitement and detective work has got his super excited. They are starting in a mall since it was a great place to people watch and still cool outside to do to much work. JCPenney's, Macy's and The Gap Store were three stores they were observing for a while now. This work is just minor thief work for the stores, they are to report to the mall security if any funny behavior or suspicious looking people are shopping at the mall. It is not much but just to prevent crime was an exciting and fun thing to start doing having little security help for these larger stores at the mall.

10

Cottage Zoo Neighbors

Henry is sitting on the cottage steps wondering who is talking. Two men beyond the trees sitting on a picnic table near the cottage next door. Something about building a small zoo on another friend's property further up-north in Traverse City. A zoo for terminally -ill children. "Wow I'm glad I brought my recorder camera with a voice recorder on it." This might be some valuable information and give us a clue to these weird sounds we have been hearing around the cottage area. Every summer next door to Henries parent's cottage all different noises have been heard. Last summer we heard sounds almost like zebras or horse sounds. Another building sounds of cats or leopard sounds. A last building sounded like peacocks or some type of bird noises. Parker and I tried to peak through the windows of one of the small buildings. We saw pink and bright yellow feathers through the windows.

Overhearing more conversations that they were soon going to transport something by Lake Huron up to Alpena,

Michigan. Then by trucks they were to transport these animals to Traverse City, Mi. where this so- called zoo was being built. The men were planning to transport the animals by fall before the lake froze.

Hearing even more talking he was not sure his tape would hold out. Taking pictures would be difficult. Being so far away and darkness was coming fast. His notebook would have to do for now.

Is this even legal transporting animals by water? He hoped his ink pen would not run out. His hands were getting sore but he has to keep writing he thought for the Junior Detective group and maybe even Uncle Al and Jerry would want to hear this information. The men continued. They were going to take the large crates and boat them up to the city of Alpena. Next a friend of the neighbors, Tom, would meet them with a rental-U-Haul. Boarding most of the crated animals onto the truck to his friend's 12- acre property. This was going to be big and wonderful. Building this zoo for terminally -ill children to come and see. A man named Jack he overheard has a daughter that was diagnosed at 7 with terminal cancer. The one man told the other man that Jack told him with great emotion and tears in his eyes about his daughter Emma. The one thing that she loved above anything else in the world was animals. As sick as she was, she fought hard just to go to a see the animals. The closest zoo was so far to go for her family. Jack has planned this for two years for Emma and other sick children. The smile and happiness this gives his daughter is a feeling he will always treasure. He even took a second job and a second loan out to build this zoo. Her love of animals was her world and what she lived for every day. Jack's love for his daughter was beyond any bond I have ever see. Jack also told him, if this will give her happiness, maybe other kids terminally ill would enjoy this zoo to give them Joy and hope for another day.

Overhearing more information, Henry had to open another notebook. Jack, the owner of the property talking about how he has a cousin who works at a small zoo in Cincinnati, Ohio. They are in the process of closing. "My wife is an animal vet", said Jack. We want to buy as many animals as possible and open our own zoo. "Wow", awesome idea!! But only a few of my friends, you and my wife know about it. I want to keep it a secret until I have it all built. Which will be very soon. He was so excited to tell his friend his news. Tears were almost coming down his face. Ouch, my hand is getting sore with all these notes. Hoping his second pen would hold out having enough ink was the answer. Henry stood to stretch hoping he would not be seen.

My wife Maggie has inherited her parent's property. Both parents were suddenly killed in a terrible car crash this past winter on some really slick roads. She is still quite upset about loosing her parents. They were so good to Emma and us it will take a while to adjust to their being gone. The property is located very close to Traverse City. It sits on 12 acres of land. Emma was their pride and joy. I think they will be so happy for us to build this zoo for Emma and all other terminally ill-cancer ridden children. Great idea, "let me know what I can do". Jack told him he could help with some of the final building work if he wants to help.

I have just rented this property for the last few summers hear in Harbor Beach. To keep the animals and slowly take them over to some of the buildings as they are being built for them to live in for the Zoo.

My cousin has inherited many of the animals from the closing zoo.

My cousin's wife's father is ill and needs to have him take care of the animals if possible. As he told me this it was perfect opportunity for filling up my zoo. My cousin worked at the zoo for twenty years now. He became part owner over the past few years. Never in my life did I think I could even find this many animals for my zoo at such a low cost. Mostly transportation and food cost for the animals that is all that is involved in getting the animals for my zoo. My cousin has agreed with moving the animals and hire on some caretakers that the animals know.

This is going to be an all- day event, thought Henry taking notes and listening to this plan. How this will and when take place is going to be quite the task of these neighbor cottage mysterious men with animals.

We have most of the barns and buildings built and newly permitted. We have a few more animals to bring over to the cottages.

Tomorrow-morning we will transport the Zebra's, peacocks and tigers. A few of the zoo workers that know these animals and how to handle them will arrive early tomorrow. They are coming from Cincinnati to transport them onto the boats. Then the boats will carry them as far as Alpena and once there, the trucks will transport them west to the new property near Traverse City.

These two men will also be bringing butterflies, three miniature horses and yes three giraffes. "Butterflies yes, the most favorite sight to see for my daughter Emma.

We will clean up all the vacant buildings next to the cottage and store the butterflies and miniature horses. The giraffes will have to be taken directly to our property. These cottages are not large enough to store giraffes. We did build an extremely tall building for the security and safety for the giraffes. We will have to transport the animals around midnight so the neighbors will not see us moving them. I am not sure it is legal to transport animals across lakes in Michigan, he said.

I want all this transporting to go well. I am hoping to open the zoo by early this fall.

Henry and Parker's eyes popped wide-open looking at each other with amazement and exhaustion. Shock and disbelief!!! Three hours of notes and conversation. "I think it is time for lunch ", I am so hungry I could eat a horse, said David. Well maybe not a horse!!! As they both almost fell over laughing walking into the cottage to eat lunch. Animals are in those small buildings we were right.

Two years of hearing strange noises. All the pieces are beginning to fall together, said Parker. Yes, two summers of wondering and detecting for the Junior Detective Club. We will have to take all our photos and note taking back to the next meeting to tell Ben and the rest of the Club. The mysterious neighbors of the north in Harbor Beach, Michigan may soon be solved.

Traverse City Zoo

Henry ran back to pick up his camera he must have dropped nearby a large Oak Tree. So many acorns, it was hard to be quiet.

The two men were still talking. Henry was still taking more notes in case of any harm or criminal activity may be planning. He could not help but listen just a little while longer.

The man named Jack was telling the two other men about the construction of the animal buildings. Henry remembered to push the video on his camera this time. He was trying to get close enough to get as many pictures of these men as possible. His Uncle Al might be interested in these men.

"The heaters' in the building will help keep the animals warm in the winter time at the zoo. The camera Henry was using were infra-red and took video and voice taping in the dark.

Jack was saying how close the buildings were to

being finished. Regulating the heat in the buildings, and purchasing each individual animals' preference of food was all that needed to be done.

The final concern Jack had was the butterfly habitat. We are calling in a specialist, called an Aviator. They know how to regulate humidity for the butterflies, trees, and flowers. For survival the temperature has to be just right. As Jack continued to talk, he said his cousin knows of a company that can give well needed help for the Butterfly habitat.

Bill another friend of Jacks added to the conversation that he was so glad to be almost done with the building of the zoo. As the rest all gave high fives to Jack and they all smiled.

It will be terrific to see it finished. "I would not miss it for the world", said Bill as they all agreed. "I would be honored to have you all come on opening day". Bill, I had a big question to ask you. Since you have helped me so much in this process of moving most of the animals, and have so much knowledge. "I would like to offer you a job."!

Really, wow said Bill. "I really love animals and worked at the other zoo for over 15 years now". "Awesome, thank-you Jack I would love to come work for you and your new zoo. I am free now and have no family I'm responsible for so I can move as soon as I sell my house.

Traverse City I've heard is beautiful, but chilly in the winter. Having the animals and Lake Michigan and a few good friends what more can a single man ask for in life" "Great said Jack. It is a beautiful area. Fresh Northern Air, delicious Lake fish to eat and every summer don't forget they put on a gigantic Cherry Festival with rides, concerts Air plane air shows everything cherry and don't forget the best fire-work show around over Lake Michigan.

People come from far away to see this beautiful city. The Cherry Festival has every kind of food imaginable, made with their terrific delicious cherries grown right in the area. They have rides for kids Ferris wheel, bumper cars, mini roller coaster, merry -go-around rides. Magic-shows, music concerts, and if you need to buy a boat they have them displayed right on the grass near the beach. College student's roller blade, bike, and walk along a long black top path. The best for us is the magnificent fish. Walleye, white fish, Orange Roughy, perch, even pike have been found in Lake Michigan. The Walleye and White fish are the best around. Tender, flaky and so tasty. "Stop, you are making me so hungry", said his friend. It is a festival that draws in people from all over the United States. I believe it goes for 2 weeks at the 20th of June and ends on the fourth with a great Fire work show on the night of July 4th.

I think this festival will be a great way to advertise our zoo. I will have to call the city and see about putting up a banner near the festival to remind new comers to visit our new zoo. I want to call it Emma's Children Zoo (for terminally ill children and family).

This has been a long building process, but I think with time and great help this zoo will put a smile on many sick children's face. Having a terminally ill child sure has opened my eyes and heart. I thank you and hope to see you soon when the mini-giraffes and miniature ponies and lastly the butterflies should arrive in 3-4 hours. Better get some shut-eye. We have got a long boat ride ahead of us. I will text you when they arrive around 12:30 am. "Okay see you soon, said Bill".

The camera battery just clicked off, Henry captured a lot of Video on his camera of Jack and Bills conversation. "Wow", Henry thought this is going to be quite a conversation to play back for Ben and the Junior Detective Club members after Easter break. As Henry made sure both men were off the boat and Bill left in a car and Jack entered the main cottage and the lights were off for the night. Henry ran as fast as he could to his parents Cottage porch. Parker was just finishing notes of the days spying. Henry was out of breath. "Wow, great work Parker said to Henry that Infrared camera sure does come in handy for great detective work, well done. Let's call it a night wow, we will have to set our alarms for 12:15 to see the animals and capture new video on my camera after I charge it up for a few hours. I think this detective work is going to be very interesting in taping the early morning delivery and boat launch. The next meeting showing video tape possibly to my Uncle Al and the Junior Detective group.

It was late at night and Henry was trying to record one last conversation. The two men were still at the boat. As the sky was very dark Parker noticed Henry was not back to the cottage porch. Parker snuck up to find Henry, but he was not there. Was Henry taken by those men? It had to be 2 or 3 in the morning. The sun would be up soon. Parker ran close to the water near the boat. Suddenly, Parker saw Henry being pulled onto the boat with the two men. "Kidnapped, oh no thought Parker". He ran pack to the cottage as fast as he could. He was exhausted, 3:30 on his watch what should I do, he thought. Parker was exhausted with fear and all the fresh night northern air he fell asleep. Parkers head lamp was still on as he dreamed of the boat slowly pulling away from shore with Henry and the other men from the next- door cottage.

Morning came and Parker knew he had to get help." Henry had been kidnapped.

Henry was frightened as the boat was speeding away. The two men said" we are not going to hurt you"." We just want to keep this a secret until it is all finished." "Oh, said Henry, what is finished.? We are building a Zoo for terminally-ill children. Jack told Henry the whole story about opening a zoo soon. Henry had questions about the animals. Jack told him they were not harming any of the animals. We were only moving them from one zoo to another where they will be safe, protected and well fed. We are moving the animals from a zoo in Cincinnati, Ohio that is closing to Traverse City, Michigan.

Parker was getting more worried as Henry was no-where in sight. It was almost 5 in the morning. Parker was so tired still from staying awake most of the night, as he thought just a few more minutes of sleep he would get help for Henry.

As Parker started to drift off for some long- needed rest he was dreaming. No, he thought as he was hearing a boat motor coming closer to shore. Parker fumbled for his infra-red binoculars and ran to a near by tree. It was Henry, thank God he thought. Henry climbed out and shook the man's hand. "It was strange thought Parker shaking his hand.

Seeing a bouncing light in the dark. Henry came running back to the cottage, yes it truly was Henry safe at last thought Parker.

"Are you okay asked Parker? Parker ran catch Henry staggering with exhaustion staying up all night was tiring. "I thought you were kidnapped, I almost woke up your parents, to call your Uncle Al." Glad you are okay, it's all okay? It is, I will tell you the whole story tomorrow. Let's get some shut-eye. I'm exhausted, me too, said Parker.

They both fell onto there cots coving up in their sleeping bags. Too exhausted to shut-off their flashlights still beaming in the morning darkness. It was almost sunrise in Harbor Beach, Michigan once again.

Opening day of the zoo was going to be extra special. All visitors would be given animal kites. The second visit, each family would receive ½ off admission price and a free zoo animal cup, color of their choice. Every animal had a cup with its own color. The Zebras were black cups, the Giraffes were yellow cups, the birds were blue, tigers were orange cups, peacocks were purple- colored cups, the miniature ponies were brown and lastly the butterfly cups were florescent lime-green.

Jack and Bill told us to keep all this a secret. Emma's Cancer Children's Zoo was going to give sixty percent of all ticket money to the cancer hospital. The opening day was 2 weeks away September 10.

12

Spring Meeting at the Park

It was almost May in Madison, Michigan. The 1st meeting at the park was this Saturday. The Junior Detective Club was excited to share this past- years detective discoveries in the city and up-north in Harbor Beach. Ben, Josh, Jenny, Henry and Parker and a few other new members had lots to share.

Observing and watching the creepy, boarded up house this past fall and winter we really found out lots of mysterious clues.

So- far many- colored bags of money have been found. Around the house and on the trail leading to the house in the city. All different dollar bill amounts were found. Twenty-dollar bill bags, fifty-dollar bill bags and one-Hundred-dollar bill bags each full of money.

The meeting was over as many members were shocked by the new findings near the creepy house.

Ben was at the hardware store getting the last items for his mom on the list. He heard to men talking in a funny whispery tone. The assistant manager Joe was talking with Mr. Jones. Overhearing the conversation, Joe said to Mr. Jones all this counterfeit money will help me open my own hardware store down in Ohio, "No more taking orders from any boss". Freedom at last. Once you are done printing up to a million dollars in sorted counterfeit money, we can open our own hardware store. "Yes, Mr. Jones said with a bad studder, "that that will be wonderful". I will be done in 1 more week. I appreciate the offer

To work at the new store, said Jim Jones. The cracked open door gave all the information Ben needed, to tell the police. As Ben grabbed Jen and they left the hardware store, he wrote down the date, place, and time and the information he heard in a back office of the store. We will have to tell the police before a week is over and Mr. Jones and Joe the assistant manager get away with all the fake money, they are laundering.

Ben and Jenny, Henry, Parker and Josh spoke with the police and Ben and Jenny's Uncle Al. "Wow, Uncle Al said, "If all this information is true this creepy boarded up house mystery will be finally solved."I will send two detectives over with a warrant to search the premises. Additionally, set up a stake out to watch for this mysterious Mr. Jim Jones. Within 3 days Jim Jones appeared late at night apparently to run his counterfeit money machine once again. Jim Jones was arrested on the spot at the sight of the machine spitting out One- Hundred- dollar bills in the basement. Down at the station Mr. Jim Jones told his whole story. He even mentioned what the money was to be used for with Joe the assistant manager. Everything began to make sense. All the colored bags of money to start up the new hardware store.

offer to work at the new store, said Mr. Jones. The cracked open door gave all the information Ben needed. As he grabbed Jen and they left the hardware he wrote down the date., place and time and all the information he heard in the back office in his notebook. We will definitely let the police know before a week is over. No way will we let Joe the assistant manager and Mr. Jones get away with all that fake money they are laundering.

Ben, Jenny, Henry, Parker, and Josh all talked to the police and Ben and Jenny's Uncle Al. "Wow, Uncle Al said, "If all this information is true, this creepy boarded up house mystery will finally be solved."

I will send two detectives over with a warrant to search the premises. Additionally set up a stake-out to watch for this mysterious Mr. Jones. Within 3 days Jim Jones appeared late at night. Apparently to run his counterfeit machine once again.

Mr. Jim Jones was arrested on the spot at the sight of the machine spitting out one hundred-dollar bills in the basement. Down at the station Mr. Jones told his whole story. He even mentioned what the money was being used for with Joe the assistant hardware store manager. Everything began to make sense. The colored bags

Of money to start up the hardware. The use of all the money would be used to purchase the supplies to be sold at the hardware. "Boy this guy Uncle Al said, told us a name of Joe Johnson who was in on it the whole time. They were each going in buying a new hardware down in Ohio. He told us so much information these two guys were going to go away to jail for a long-long time."

13

Spring Once Again

It was the beginning of May and the Junior Detective Club was having their final meeting of the school year.

Henry and Parker have just informed the group of the up-north Harbor Beach investigation. Strange noises in the middle of summer inside 4 to 5 mini cabins next door. All seemed to be of animal sounds.

The Zoo for Terminally -Ill Children was not finished yet. The zoo in Cincinnati had just closed and Jack needed some-where to shelter the animals for his new zoo. Four mini cottages were built with food and water for temporary shelter. Jack and his zoo crew were frantically finishing the shelters on his new land for each animal. He inherited this land from a relative that had recently passed away.

Ben spoke up and knew of a few kids that unfortunately have relatives with cancer and are terminally ill. Jenny decided to have a banner made announcing the opening time and day of the new zoo in Traverse City. "Yes, great idea said, Ben." We can make up flyers and pass them around to local schools. Another idea might be to put flyers up in the city library or community center to help Jack announce the zoo opening. After getting paper and colorful supplies together Henry and Parker were both thinking out loud. Parker said, "The Junior Detective Club can be more than always finding crime in neighborhoods. We can team up with families in our elementary, middle school, and high school to give to the zoo or even give to surrounding cancer families and hospitals. One way would be to have a twice a month bake sales at each school. A portion of the sales would of course, go to the school, but maybe sixty percent of these bake sales could go to the zoo or local hospitals in the cancer wing for children. Also, money could be raised to help pay for gas, travel and hotel money to visit the zoo in Traverse City.

Jenny agreed and said, we should set up a meeting before school gets out with the principal and get these fundraising ideas finalized before the end of school. Hoping a larger portion can be donated to the zoo or cancer wings in hospitals. The animals will need care and food so maybe we can work this out between the principal and our detective club soon. Great idea we will all think about some other fundraiser ideas for the cancer families at the hospitals or money for the zoo. School will be out in a month. We had 1 week to come up with more fundraisers. Maybe used book sales or gently used clothes from parents at each school to sell as fundraisers ideas.

The Vice Principal cleared a final bake sale for June tenth, 5 days before school was out. The high school, middle school and elementary schools were all okayed for bake sales. Jen and Parker worked on the high school and middle school flyers and Henry and Ben worked on the elementary flyers. There would be a flyer put in each hallway in all classrooms on the front doors to each school. A sign- up sheet attached. Brownies, chocolate chip cookies, sugar cookies, oatmeal cookies, M and M cookies, and many cupcakes were donated for each sale. Cinnamon cream cheese cupcakes, chocolate muffins, and Blueberry Muffins, "My favorite, said Jenny." These kinds of muffins were all donated for the sale. It was so kind of the parents to see so many items being donated for all 3 sales. All kinds of bagels were also brought in 3 dozen to be exact. Families were so excited to help raise money for the zoo and hospitals for cancer kids. Many families were planning their trips up to Traverse City to see the new zoo.

14

Final Weeks of School

Junior High School for Josh and Jenny were almost done for the end of their school year. Ben, Henry and Parker's high school year had one more week to go until summer. They would all be going into there final year at Madison High School. "Senior year awesome thought Ben."

The money raised for cancer families, Emma's Zoo and the hospital was a very good start. It was all divided into three areas.

Henry received a text on his phone a few days after school was out.

"It was Jack the zoo owner." He has invited the whole Junior Detective Club for a sneak peak of Emma's Zoo. Jack says it is getting finished earlier than expected.

Great Henry replied, "whoever can make it up to Traverse City will definitely come to see Emma's Zoo.

"Ben added, "Great we will take up the zoo portion of the fundraising money and surprise Jack and Emma.

Henry's Uncle Paul worked at the local Traverse City Paper. He was doing a small story on the new Zoo opening near town. He wanted to get a picture of the Junior Detective Club helping out the new Zoo plus giving donations from school fundraisers to cancer kids in local hospitals.

The fundraisers were going to be divided up fifty-percent sales were going to Emma's Zoo and fifty-percent going to local hospitals with sick cancer children.

We had 8 cars of club members able to go see the zoo. Including the parents, volunteering to drive. Some of us members did not all have our drivers license yet.

Arriving at the zoo we saw the biggest sign lit up in bright florescent lights. Emma's Zoo in purple and pink gigantic letters. Jack said those are her favorite colors. We were all given large purple drink glasses full of pink lemonade. Sunglasses any color of our choice.

Large wooden signs with arrows pointing to each animal exhibit. Each animal sign was color coded to make it very colorful. Emma's favorite things are very bright colors, pink lemonade, cookies and balloons. Her favorite animal is the colorful butterflies. Colors are really what makes her smile the most, well besides her parents and close friends. All of us in the Junior Detective Club thought each animal exhibit was beautifully set up. Many of the animal areas had lower- level petting and feeding areas for wheel chair height access. The miniature ponies loved to be fed carrots and sugar cubes.

We noticed hand noticed any hand rails placed around the zoo would help those kids that needed support. Florescent rails of yellow and lime green were installed at many areas of the zoo. Some kids may not be in wheel chairs. Support rails would help those with balance issues or leg or feet issues. So many handicap support areas ramps, wide entrances, support rails and open seating for wheel chair access at concession areas at the tables were put into place. Even in the restroom areas wide stalls lower sink, towel, and soap access were also installed. They had two areas for renting wheel chairs if needed. Just $2.00 a day to rent. Emma wanted the wheel chair sign to be read in florescent pink. Emma loves florescent pink. Every child would receive a balloon and keep sake cup, any color of their choice. The last item for them as they leave would be ½ off ticket on their return visit to the zoo.

Every animal area was color coded. The Butterfly area was bright yellow, the miniature ponies were light blue, the giraffes were orange and the Lions and Tigers were red signs. At Emma's request all signs were painted in florescent colored paint big with all capital letters so not to be lost. Easy access in and around the zoo was done especially for all the families to accommodate them at the zoo.

Jack could not have been happier to receive all the donated money we raised at the school. It was not a lot but $850.00 would truly help with animal help and upkeep of the zoo for a season.

All of us that came up had felt so happy for Jack and Emma's new Zoo. The animals looked safe and very happy in their new environment. Plenty of food, shelter and open land helped all the animals settle into their new homes at the zoo. "The walkways were just poured one week ago, Jack said." Colored foot prints of each animal led visitors to an animal exhibit. A little extra money was used to cement the walkways for easier access for wheel-chair passage around the zoo. Walkers, crutches, and wheel chair users would all have a smooth and easier paths throughout the zoo. A large parking lot addition was just poured and dried a few days ago. Large spots for Vans and Busses were drawn out in the lot for easy parking .

Printed in the United States
by Baker & Taylor Publisher Services